2

To my wife

First published in Picture Lions in 1996
1 3 5 7 9 10 8 6 4 2
Picture Lions is an imprint of the Children's Division, part of HarperCollins Publishers Ltd,
77-85 Fulham Palace Road, Hammersmith, London W6 8JB.
First published in Great Britain by HarperCollins Publishers Ltd in 1996
Text and illustrations copyright © John Wallace 1996
The author/illustrator asserts the moral right to be identified as the author/illustrator of the work.
A CIP catalogue for this title is available from the British Library.
ISBN: 0 00 664581 X

Little Bean

John Wallace

PictureLions

An Imprint of HarperCollins*Publishers*

Please can I have a story?

Not now, Little Bean,
your father is tired.

Come away, your father is busy.

He has to go away tomorrow.

Will he read me a story before he goes?

Only if you're awake.

Where's Daddy?

He had to go early, darling.
He's going to be very busy.

Well, I can be busy too!
Busy! Busy! Busy!

Busy playing ball

busy having lunch

 busy answering the phone

busy feeding Oscar

 busy playing

busy brushing my teeth

busy saying goodnight.

But at the end of the day she said,
"I wonder where my Daddy is?"

Little Bean's Daddy was busy.

Busy at meetings

busy eating

busy phoning

busy reading

busy writing

busy getting ready for bed

busy brushing his teeth.

But at the end of the day he said,
"I wonder what my Little Bean is
doing right now?"

The next evening he stopped
at a bookshop

and then he hurried home.

Little Bean was fast asleep,

but not for long!

Here are some more Picture Lions

for you to enjoy